Sofia the First

The Amulet and the Anthem

Written by Catherine Hapka • Based on an episode by Matt Boren

Illustrated by Character Building Studio and the Disney Storybook Artists

DISNEY PRESS

New York • Los Angeles

Today is a special day in Enchancia. Sofia is at the stadium with Jade and Ruby.

"Every kid in the kingdom is here!" Sofia exclaims.

"Being chosen to sing the Enchancian anthem at the Harvest Festival is a big deal," Ruby says.

Ruby and Jade both hope their names will be chosen in the drawing. They practice singing the anthem together while they wait. "You two sound amazing!" Sofia cries.

Luciano, the host of the event, takes the stage.
"It's the moment you've been waiting for," he says.
"This year's singer will be . . ." Luciano picks a name
out of a drum. "Princess Sofia!"

"Congratulations!" Jade says. Ruby gives Sofia a big hug. Then Luciano calls her up onstage.

"Go on, Sofia!" Ruby says. "We'll wait for you."

Sofia can't believe she was chosen.

"Thank you!" she says, waving to the crowd. "This is so exciting!"

Luciano guides Sofia backstage.

"But my friends . . ." Sofia begins.

"This is no time for friends," Luciano says. "You are the anthem singer! You have people to meet, gifts to receive, and of course, you must rehearse the song. . . ."

After that, Sofia hardly has time
to take a breath. The painterazzi want
to paint her picture. The newspapers
want to interview her. The townspeople
shower her with gifts.

While Sofia prepares for the big day, Ruby and Jade wait for her outside.

"I'm so sorry!" Sofia cries, running up to her friends. "I couldn't get away until now."

"That's okay," Ruby says. "How was it?"

"Unbelievable!" Sofia exclaims. "They gave me this hat, and they're going to send hundreds of gowns to the castle, and . . ."

Sofia goes on and on, bragging about her day. She's so excited she doesn't notice when her friends look hurt.

She also doesn't notice when her amulet starts to glow. . . .

Sofia returns to the stage to rehearse her song. She opens her mouth to sing—but after a few words, she lets out a loud, froggy "Croak!"

Sofia isn't sure what happened. "I'm a bit tired," she tells Luciano. "But don't worry, I know 'O Enchancia' by heart."

"All right," Luciano says. "Get some rest, and we'll see you at the festival tomorrow."

"Thank you—Croak!" Sofia covers her mouth and rushes offstage.

Back at the castle, Sofia finds Clover and tells him what happened. "What do you think is—croak—wrong with me?" she cries.

Clover looks worried. "You've been cursed!" he says.

Sofia realizes only Cedric can help. When she tells him what happened, the sorcerer says her amulet must be to blame.

"I thought my amulet only gave me magical powers," Sofia says.

"How soon you forget!" Cedric clears his throat. "'With each deed performed, for better or worse, a power is granted, a blessing—or curse.'"

Sofia is stunned. "The amulet cursed me—Croak!" she tells
Clover. "Because I did something that wasn't nice."

"We've got to figure out what you did," Clover says. "Maybe that
will undo the curse."

But by the next morning, they still haven't figured it out.
"I've got an idea," Clover says at last. "We've got to hop
back—go over everything you did yesterday."

Sofia leads Clover all through the castle and then to the stadium.
She remembers Luciano calling her onstage . . .

and getting her portrait painted . . .

and being interviewed . . .

and showered with gifts.

"Then I remembered Jade and Ruby were waiting for me," Sofia says. "I ran and told them about everything. I was so excited—Croak! That's when it started."

Nearby, Sofia hears Amber bragging to her friends about the time *she* was chosen to sing the anthem.

"She sounds like . . . me!" Sofia realizes. "I was bragging to Ruby and Jade. I bet I made them feel bad, Clover. That must be why I'm cursed!"

Sofia quickly changes into her Harvest Festival gown and then runs
to find her friends. "I shouldn't have bragged about being the anthem
singer," she says. "I'm really sorry if I hurt your feelings."
To Sofia's relief, Ruby and Jade forgive her.

But after Sofia leaves her friends, she lets out another loud "Croak!"
Oh, no! It's almost time for her performance—and she's still cursed!
Sofia isn't sure what to do.
Suddenly, her amulet glows again—and Princess Belle appears!

Sofia tells Belle what happened. "Can you help me?" she asks. Belle smiles. "The only person who can undo the curse is you, Sofia," she says. "Someone I love did something unkind and was cursed, too. He looked into his heart and gave up something he wanted, to show that he was truly sorry."

Sofia thinks about Belle's words. "Look into my heart . . . give up something," she murmurs. "I think I know what to do, Belle!" But Princess Belle is already gone.

Suddenly, Sofia hears Luciano introducing her. "Hi, everyone," she says, running onstage. "I wish I could sing today. But—croak—I have a frog in my throat."

The crowd gasps.

"It's okay," Sofia says. "I wasn't—croak—nice to my friends yesterday, and I want to make it up to them. Ruby and Jade, will you come up and sing the Enchancian anthem?"

As soon as Jade and Ruby start to sing, Sofia's amulet glows once more.

"I did it!" Sofia whispers to Clover. "The curse is gone."

Then Ruby and Jade pull Sofia over to join them. And not a croak can be heard as the three friends sing every word of "O Enchancia" together.

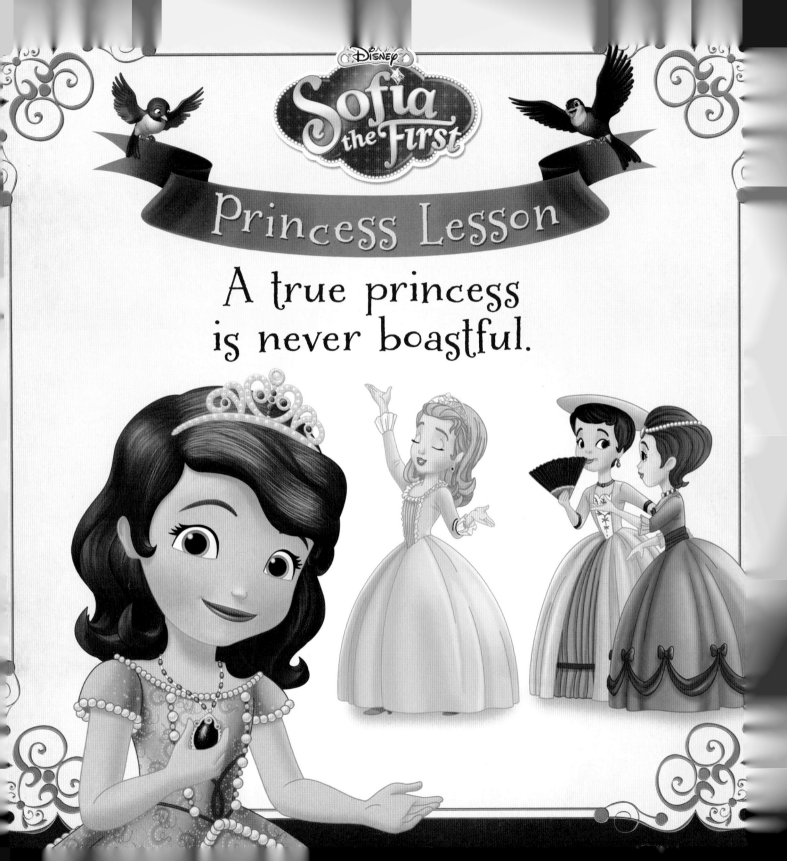

DISNEY

Sofia the First

Princess Lesson

A true princess
is never boastful.